THE CREATURES THAT
TIME FORGOT

THE CREATURES THAT TIME FORGOT

by Ray Bradbury

Mad, impossible world! Sun-blasted by day, cold-wracked by night—and life condensed by radiation into eight days! Sim eyed the Ship—if he only dared reach it and escape! ... but it was more than half an hour distant—the limit of life itself!

During the night, Sim was born. He lay wailing upon the cold cave stones. His blood beat through him a thousand pulses each minute. He grew, steadily.

Into his mouth his mother with feverish hands put the food. The nightmare of living was begun. Almost instantly at birth his eyes grew alert, and then, without half understanding why, filled with bright, insistent terror. He gagged upon the food, choked and wailed. He looked about, blindly.

There was a thick fog. It cleared. The outlines of the cave appeared. And a man loomed up, insane and wild and terrible. A man with a dying face. Old, withered by winds, baked like adobe in the heat. The man was crouched in a far corner of the cave, his eyes whitening to one side of his face, listening to the far wind trumpeting up above on the frozen night planet.

Sim's mother, trembling, now and again, staring at the man, fed Sim pebble-fruits, valley-grasses and ice-nipples broken from the cavern entrances, and eating, eliminating, eating again, he grew larger, larger.

The man in the corner of the cave was his father! The man's eyes were all that was alive in his face. He held a crude stone dagger in his withered hands and his jaw hung loose and senseless.

THE CREATURES THAT TIME FORGOT

Then, with a widening focus, Sim saw the old people sitting in the tunnel beyond this living quarter. And as he watched, they began to die.

Their agonies filled the cave. They melted like waxen images, their faces collapsed inward on their sharp bones, their teeth protruded. One minute their faces were mature, fairly smooth, alive, electric. The next minute a desication and burning away of their flesh occurred.

Sim thrashed in his mother's grasp. She held him. "No, no," she soothed him, quietly, earnestly, looking to see if this, too, would cause her husband to rise again.

With a soft swift padding of naked feet, Sim's father ran across the cave. Sim's mother screamed. Sim felt himself torn loose from her grasp. He fell upon the stones, rolling, shrieking with his new, moist lungs!

The webbed face of his father jerked over him, the knife was poised. It was like one of those prenatal nightmares he'd had while still in his mother's flesh. In the next few blazing, impossible instants questions flicked through his brain. The knife was high, suspended, ready to destroy him. But the whole question of life in this cave, the dying people, the withering and the insanity, surged through Sim's new, small head. How was it that he understood? A newborn child? Can a newborn child think, see, understand, interpret? No. It was wrong! It was impossible. Yet it was happening! To him. He had been alive an hour now. And in the next instant perhaps dead!

His mother flung herself upon the back of his father, and beat down the weapon. Sim caught the terrific backwash of emotion from both their conflicting minds. "Let me kill him!" shouted the father, breathing harshly, sobbingly. "What has he to live for?"

6

"No, no!" insisted the mother, and her body, frail and old as it was, stretched across the huge body of the father, tearing at his weapon. "He must live! There may be a future for him! He may live longer than us, and be young!"

The father fell back against a stone crib. Lying there, staring, eyes glittering, Sim saw another figure inside that stone crib. A girl-child, quietly feeding itself, moving its delicate hands to procure food. His sister.

The mother wrenched the dagger from her husband's grasp, stood up, weeping and pushing back her cloud of stiffening gray hair. Her mouth trembled and jerked. "I'll kill you!" she said, glaring down at her husband. "Leave my children alone."

The old man spat tiredly, bitterly, and looked vacantly into the stone crib, at the little girl. "One-eighth of *her* life's over, already," he gasped. "And she doesn't know it. What's the use?"

As Sim watched, his own mother seemed to shift and take a tortured, smoke-like form. The thin bony face broke out into a maze of wrinkles. She was shaken with pain and had to sit by him, shuddering and cuddling the knife to her shriveled breasts. She, like the old people in the tunnel, was aging, dying.

Sim cried steadily. Everywhere he looked was horror. A mind came to meet his own. Instinctively he glanced toward the stone crib. Dark, his sister, returned his glance. Their minds brushed like straying fingers. He relaxed somewhat. He began to learn.

The father sighed, shut his lids down over his green eyes. "Feed the child," he said, exhaustedly. "Hurry. It is almost dawn and it is our last day of living, woman. Feed him. Make him grow."

Sim quieted, and images, out of the terror, floated to him.

This was a planet next to the sun. The nights burned with cold, the days were like torches of fire. It was a violent, impossible world. The people lived in the cliffs to escape the incredible ice and the day of flame. Only at dawn and sunset was the air breath-sweet, flower-strong, and then the cave peoples brought their children out into a stony, barren valley. At dawn the ice thawed into creeks and rivers, at sunset the day-fires died and cooled. In the intervals of even, livable temperature the people lived, ran, played, loved, free of the caverns; all life on the planet jumped, burst into life. Plants grew instantly, birds were flung like pellets across the sky. Smaller, legged animal life rushed frantically through the rocks; everything tried to get its living down in the brief hour of respite.

It was an unbearable planet. Sim understood this, a matter of hours after birth. Racial memory bloomed in him. He would live his entire life in the caves, with two hours a day outside. Here, in stone channels of air he would talk, talk incessantly with his people, sleep never, think, think and lie upon his back, dreaming; but never sleeping.

And he would live exactly eight days.

*

The violence of this thought evacuated his bowels. Eight days. Eight *short* days. It was wrong, impossible, but a fact. Even while in his mother's flesh some racial knowledge had told him he was being formed rapidly, shaped and propelled out swiftly.

Birth was quick as a knife. Childhood was over in a flash. Adolescence was a sheet of lightning. Manhood was a dream, maturity a myth, old age an inescapably quick reality, death a swift certainty.

Eight days from now he'd stand half-blind, withering, dying, as his father now stood, staring uselessly at his own wife and child.

This day was an eighth part of his total life! He must enjoy every second of it. He must search his parents' thoughts for knowledge.

Because in a few hours they'd be dead.

This was so impossibly unfair. Was this all of life? In his prenatal state hadn't he dreamed of *long* lives, valleys not of blasted stone but green foliage and temperate clime? Yes! And if he'd dreamed then there must be truth in the visions. How could he seek and find the long life? Where? And how could he accomplish a life mission that huge and depressing in eight short, vanishing days?

How had his people gotten into such a condition?

As if at a button pressed, he saw an image. Metal seeds, blown across space from a distant green world, fighting with long flames, crashing on this bleak planet. From their shattered hulls tumble men and women.

When? Long ago. Ten thousand days. The crash victims hid in the cliffs from the sun. Fire, ice and floods washed away the wreckage of the huge metal seeds. The victims were shaped and beaten like iron upon a forge. Solar radiations drenched them. Their pulses quickened, two hundred, five hundred, a thousand beats a minute. Their skins thickened, their blood changed. Old age came rushing. Children were born in the caves. Swifter, swifter, swifter the process. Like all this world's wild life, the men and women from the crash lived and died in a week, leaving children to do likewise.

So this is life, thought Sim. It was not spoken in his mind, for he knew no words, he knew only images, old memory, an awareness, a telepathy that could penetrate flesh, rock, metal. So I'm the five thousandth in a long line of futile sons? What can I do to save myself from dying eight days from now? Is there escape?

His eyes widened, another image came to focus.

Beyond this valley of cliffs, on a low mountain lay a perfect, unscarred metal seed. A metal ship, not rusted or touched by the avalanches. The ship was deserted, whole, intact. It was the only ship of all these that had crashed that was still a unit, still usable. But it was so far away. There was no one in it to help. This ship, then, on the far mountain, was the destiny toward which he would grow. There was his only hope of escape.

His mind flexed.

In this cliff, deep down in a confinement of solitude, worked a handful of scientists. To these men, when he was old enough and wise enough, he must go. They, too, dreamed of escape, of long life, of green valleys and temperate weathers. They, too, stared longingly at that distant ship upon its high mountain, its metal so perfect it did not rust or age.

The cliff groaned.

Sim's father lifted his eroded, lifeless face.

"Dawn's coming," he said.

*

Morning relaxed the mighty granite cliff muscles. It was the time of the Avalanche.

The tunnels echoed to running bare feet. Adults, children pushed with eager, hungry eyes toward the outside dawn. From far out, Sim heard a rumble of rock, a scream, a silence. Avalanches fell into valley. Stones that had been biding their time, not quite ready to fall, for a million years let go their bulks, and where they had begun their journey as single boulders they smashed upon the valley floor in a thousand shrapnels and friction-heated nuggets.

Every morning at least one person was caught in the downpour.

The cliff people dared the avalanches. It added one more excitement to their lives, already too short, too headlong, too dangerous.

Sim felt himself seized up by his father. He was carried brusquely down the tunnel for a thousand yards, to where the daylight appeared. There was a shining insane light in his father's eyes. Sim could not move. He sensed what was going to happen. Behind his father, his mother hurried, bringing with her the little sister, Dark. "Wait! Be careful!" she cried to her husband.

Sim felt his father crouch, listening.

High in the cliff was a tremor, a shivering.

"Now!" bellowed his father, and leaped out.

An avalanche fell down at them!

Sim had accelerated impressions of plunging walls, dust, confusion. His mother screamed! There was a jolting, a plunging.

With one last step, Sim's father hurried him forward into the day. The avalanche thundered behind him. The mouth of the cave, where mother and Dark stood back out of the way, was choked with rubble and two boulders that weighed a hundred pounds each.

The storm thunder of the avalanche passed away to a trickle of sand. Sim's father burst out into laughter. "Made it! By the Gods! Made it alive!" And he looked scornfully at the cliff and spat. "Pagh!"

Mother and sister Dark struggled through the rubble. She cursed her husband. "Fool! You might have killed Sim!"

"I may yet," retorted the father.

Sim was not listening. He was fascinated with the remains of an avalanche afront of the next tunnel. A blood stain trickled out from under a rise of boulders, soaking into the ground. There was nothing else to be seen. Someone else had lost the game.

Dark ran ahead on lithe, supple feet, naked and certain.

The valley air was like a wine filtered between mountains. The heaven was a restive blue; not the pale scorched atmosphere of full day, nor the bloated, bruised black-purple of night, a-riot with sickly shining stars.

THE CREATURES THAT TIME FORGOT

This was a tide pool. A place where waves of varying and violent temperatures struck, receded. Now the tide pool was quiet, cool, and its life moved abroad.

Laughter! Far away, Sim heard it. Why laughter? How could any of his people find time for laughing? Perhaps later he would discover why.

The valley suddenly blushed with impulsive color. Plant-life, thawing in the precipitant dawn, shoved out from most unexpected sources. It flowered as you watched. Pale green tendrils appeared on scoured rocks. Seconds later, ripe globes of fruit twitched upon the blade-tips. Father gave Sim over to mother and harvested the momentary, volatile crop, thrust scarlet, blue, yellow fruits into a fur sack which hung at his waist. Mother tugged at the moist new grasses, laid them on Sim's tongue.

His senses were being honed to a fine edge. He stored knowledge thirstily. He understood love, marriage, customs, anger, pity, rage, selfishness, shadings and subtleties, realities and reflections. One thing suggested another. The sight of green plant life whirled his mind like a gyroscope, seeking balance in a world where lack of time for explanations made a mind seek and interpret on its own. The soft burden of food gave him knowledge of his system, of energy, of movement. Like a bird newly cracking its way from a shell, he was almost a unit, complete, all-knowing. Heredity had done all this for him. He grew excited with his ability.

*

They walked, mother, father and the two children, smelling the smells, watching the birds bounce from wall to wall of the valley like scurrying pebbles and suddenly the father said a strange thing:

"Remember?"

12

Remember what? Sim lay cradled. Was it any effort for them to remember when they'd lived only seven days!

The husband and wife looked at each other.

"Was it only three days ago?" said the woman, her body shaking, her eyes closing to think. "I can't believe it. It is so unfair." She sobbed, then drew her hand across her face and bit her parched lips. The wind played at her gray hair. "Now is my turn to cry. An hour ago it was you!"

"An hour is half a life."

"Come," she took her husband's arm. "Let us look at everything, because it will be our last looking."

"The sun'll be up in a few minutes," said the old man. "We must turn back now."

"Just one more moment," pleaded the woman.

"The sun will catch us."

"Let it catch me then!"

"You don't mean that."

"I mean nothing, nothing at all," cried the woman.

The sun was coming fast. The green in the valley burnt away. Searing wind blasted from over the cliffs. Far away where sun bolts hammered battlements of cliff, the huge stone faces shook their contents; those avalanches not already powdered down, were now released and fell like mantles.

"Dark!" shouted the father. The girl sprang over the warm floor of the valley, answering, her hair a black flag behind her. Hands full of green fruits, she joined them.

The sun rimmed the horizon with flame, the air convulsed dangerously with it, and whistled.

The cave people bolted, shouting, picking up their fallen children, bearing vast loads of fruit and grass with them back to their deep hideouts. In moments the valley was bare. Except for one small child someone had forgotten. He was running far out on the flatness, but he was not strong enough, and the engulfing heat was drifting down from the cliffs even as he was half across the valley.

Flowers were burnt into effigies, grasses sucked back into rocks like singed snakes, flower seeds whirled and fell in the sudden furnace blast of wind, sown far into gullies and crannies, ready to blossom at sunset tonight, and then go to seed and die again.

Sim's father watched that child running, alone, out on the floor of the valley. He and his wife and Dark and Sim were safe in the mouth of their tunnel.

"He'll never make it," said father. "Do not watch him, woman. It's not a good thing to watch."

They turned away. All except Sim, whose eyes had caught a glint of metal far away. His heart hammered in him, and his eyes blurred. Far away, atop a low mountain, one of those metal seeds from space reflected a dazzling ripple of light! It was like one of his intra-embryo dreams fulfilled! A metal space seed, intact, undamaged, lying on a mountain! There was his future! There was his hope for survival! There was where he would go in a few days, when he was—strange thought—a grown man!

The sun plunged into the valley like molten lava.

The little running child screamed, the sun burned, and the screaming stopped.

Sim's mother walked painfully, with sudden age, down the tunnel, paused, reached up, broke off two last icicles that had formed during the night. She handed one to her husband, kept the other. "We will drink one last toast. To you, to the children."

"To *you*," he nodded to her. "To the children." They lifted the icicles. The warmth melted the ice down into their thirsty mouths.

RAY BRADBURY

*

All day the sun seemed to blaze and erupt into the valley. Sim could not see it, but the vivid pictorials in his parents' minds were sufficient evidence of the nature of the day fire. The light ran like mercury, sizzling and roasting the caves, poking inward, but never penetrating deeply enough. It lighted the caves. It made the hollows of the cliff comfortably warm.

Sim fought to keep his parents young. But no matter how hard he fought with mind and image, they became like mummies before him. His father seemed to dissolve from one stage of oldness to another. This is what will happen to me soon, though Sim in terror.

Sim grew upon himself. He felt the digestive-eliminatory movements of his body. He was fed every minute, he was continually swallowing, feeding. He began to fit words to images and processes. Such a word was love. It was not an abstraction, but a process, a stir of breath, a smell of morning air, a flutter of heart, the curve of arm holding him, the look in the suspended face of his mother. He saw the processes, then searched behind her suspended face and there was the word, in her brain, ready to use. His throat prepared to speak. Life was pushing him, rushing him along toward oblivion.

He sensed the expansion of his fingernails, the adjustments of his cells, the profusion of his hair, the multiplication of his bones and sinew, the grooving of the soft pale wax of his brain. His brain at birth as clear as a circle of ice, innocent, unmarked, was, an instant later, as if hit with a thrown rock, cracked and marked and patterned in a million crevices of thought and discovery.

His sister, Dark, ran in and out with other little hothouse children, forever eating. His mother trembled over him, not eating, she had no appetite, her eyes were webbed shut.

"Sunset," said his father, at last.

15

THE CREATURES THAT TIME FORGOT

The day was over. The light faded, a wind sounded.

His mother arose. "I want to see the outside world once more ... just once more...." She stared blindly, shivering.

His father's eyes were shut, he lay against the wall.

"I cannot rise," he whispered faintly. "I cannot."

"Dark!" The mother croaked, the girl came running. "Here," and Sim was handed to the girl. "Hold to Sim, Dark, feed him, care for him." She gave Sim one last fondling touch.

Dark said not a word, holding Sim, her great green eyes shining wetly.

"Go now," said the mother. "Take him out into the sunset time. Enjoy yourselves. Pick foods, eat. Play."

Dark walked away without looking back. Sim twisted in her grasp, looking over her shoulder with unbelieving, tragic eyes. He cried out and somehow summoned from his lips the first word of his existence.

"Why...?"

He saw his mother stiffen. "The child spoke!"

"Aye," said his father. "Did you hear what he said?"

"I heard," said the mother quietly.

The last thing Sim saw of his living parents was his mother weakly, swayingly, slowly moving across the floor to lie beside her silent husband. That was the last time he ever saw them move.

*

The night came and passed and then started the second day.

The bodies of all those who had died during the night were carried in a funeral procession to the top of a small hill. The procession was long, the bodies numerous.

Dark walked in the procession, holding the newly walking Sim by one hand. Only an hour before dawn Sim had learned to walk.

At the top of the hill, Sim saw once again the far off metal seed. Nobody ever looked at it, or spoke of it. Why? Was there some reason? Was it a mirage? Why did they not run toward it? Worship it? Try to get to it and fly away into space?

The funeral words were spoken. The bodies were placed upon the ground where the sun, in a few minutes, would cremate them.

The procession then turned and ran down the hill, eager to have their few minutes of free time running and playing and laughing in the sweet air.

Dark and Sim, chattering like birds, feeding among the rocks, exchanged what they knew of life. He was in his second day, she in her third. They were driven, as always, by the mercurial speed of their lives.

Another piece of his life opened wide.

Fifty young men ran down from the cliffs, holding sharp stones and rock daggers in their thick hands. Shouting, they ran off toward distant black, low lines of small rock cliffs.

"War!"

The thought stood in Sim's brain. It shocked and beat at him. These men were running to fight, to kill, over there in those small black cliffs where other people lived.

But why? Wasn't life short enough without fighting, killing?

From a great distance he heard the sound of conflict, and it made his stomach cold. "Why, Dark, why?"

Dark didn't know. Perhaps they would understand tomorrow. Now, there was the business of eating to sustain and support their lives. Watching Dark was like seeing a lizard forever flickering its pink tongue, forever hungry.

THE CREATURES THAT TIME FORGOT

Pale children ran on all sides of them. One beetle-like boy scuttled up the rocks, knocking Sim aside, to take from him a particularly luscious red berry he had found growing under an outcrop.

The child ate hastily of the fruit before Sim could gain his feet. Then Sim hurled himself unsteadily, the two of them fell in a ridiculous jumble, rolling, until Dark pried them, squalling, apart.

Sim bled. A part of him stood off, like a god, and said, "This should not be. Children should not be this way. It is wrong!"

Dark slapped the little intruding boy away. "Get on!" she cried. "What's your name, bad one?"

"Chion!" laughed the boy. "Chion, Chion, Chion!"

Sim glared at him with all the ferocity in his small, unskilled features. He choked. This was his enemy. It was as if he'd waited for an enemy of person as well as scene. He had already understood the avalanches, the heat, the cold, the shortness of life, but these were things of places, of scene—mute, extravagant manifestations of unthinking nature, not motivated save by gravity and radiation. Here, now, in this stridulent Chion he recognized a thinking enemy!

Chion darted off, turned at a distance, tauntingly crying:

"Tomorrow I will be big enough to kill you!"

And he vanished around a rock.

More children ran, giggling, by Sim. Which of them would be friends, enemies? How could friends and enemies come about in this impossible, quick life time? There was no time to make either, was there?

Dark, as if knowing his thoughts, drew him away. As they searched for desired foods, she whispered fiercely in his ear. "Enemies are made over things like stolen foods; gifts of long grasses make friends. Enemies come, too, from opinions and thoughts. In five seconds you've made an enemy for life. Life's so short enemies must be made

18

quickly." And she laughed with an irony strange for one so young, who was growing older before her rightful time. "You must fight to protect yourself. Others, superstitious ones, will try killing you. There is a belief, a ridiculous belief, that if one kills another, the murderer partakes of the life energy of the slain, and therefore will live an extra day. You see? As long as that is believed, you're in danger."

But Sim was not listening. Bursting from a flock of delicate girls who tomorrow would be tall, quieter, and who day after that would gain breasts and the next day take husbands, Sim caught sight of one small girl whose hair was a violet blue flame.

She ran past, brushed Sim, their bodies touched. Her eyes, white as silver coins, shone at him. He knew then that he'd found a friend, a love, a wife, one who'd a week from now lie with him atop the funeral pyre as sunlight undressed their flesh from bone.

Only the glance, but it held them in mid-motion, one instant.

"Your name?" he shouted after her.

"Lyte!" she called laughingly back.

"I'm Sim," he answered, confused and bewildered.

"Sim!" she repeated it, flashing on. "I'll remember!"

Dark nudged his ribs. "Here, *eat*," she said to the distracted boy. "Eat or you'll never get big enough to catch her."

From nowhere, Chion appeared, running by. "Lyte!" he mocked, dancing malevolently along and away. "Lyte! I'll remember Lyte, too!"

Dark stood tall and reed slender, shaking her dark ebony clouds of hair, sadly. "I see your life before you, little Sim. You'll need weapons soon to fight for this Lyte one. Now, hurry—the sun's coming!"

They ran back to the caves.

*

One-fourth of his life was over! Babyhood was gone. He was now a young boy! Wild rains lashed the valley at nightfall. He watched new river channels cut in the valley, out past the mountain of the metal seed. He stored the knowledge for later use. Each night there was a new river, a bed newly cut.

"What's beyond the valley?" wondered Sim.

"No one's ever been beyond it," explained Dark. "All who tried to reach the plain were frozen to death or burnt. The only land we know's within half an hour's run. Half an hour out and half an hour back."

"No one has ever reached the metal seed, then?"

Dark scoffed. "The Scientists, they try. Silly fools. They don't know enough to stop. It's no use. It's too far."

The Scientists. The word stirred him. He had almost forgotten the vision he had short hours after birth. His voice was eager. "Where are the Scientists?" he demanded.

Dark looked away from him, "I wouldn't tell you if I knew. They'd kill you, experimenting! I don't want you joining them! Live your life, don't cut it in half trying to reach that silly metal thing on the mountain."

"I'll find out where they are from someone else, then!"

"No one'll tell you! They hate the Scientists. You'll have to find them on your own. And then what? Will you save us? Yes, save us, little boy!" Her face was sullen; already half her life was gone, her breasts were beginning to shape. Tomorrow she must divine how best to live her youth, her love, and she knew no way to fully plumb the depths of passion in so short a space.

"We can't sit and talk and eat," he protested. "And *nothing* else."

"There's always love," she retorted acidly. "It helps one forget. Gods, yes," she spat it out. "Love!"

*

20

Sim ran through the tunnels, seeking. Sometimes he half imagined where the Scientists were. But then a flood of angry thought from those around him, when he asked the direction to the Scientists' cave, washed over him in confusion and resentment. After all, it was the Scientists' fault that they had been placed upon this terrible world! Sim flinched under the bombardment of oaths and curses.

Quietly he took his seat in a central chamber with the children to listen to the grown men talk. This was the time of education, the Time of Talking. No matter how he chafed at delay, or how great his impatience, even though life slipped fast from him and death approached like a black meteor, he knew his mind needed knowledge. Tonight, then, was the night of school. But he sat uneasily. Only *five* more days of life.

Chion sat across from Sim, his thin-mouthed face arrogant.

Lyte appeared between the two. The last few hours had made her firmer footed, gentler, taller. Her hair shone brighter. She smiled as she sat beside Sim, ignoring Chion. And Chion became rigid at this and ceased eating.

The dialogue crackled, filled the room. Swift as heart beats, one thousand, two thousand words a minute. Sim learned, his head filled. He did not shut his eyes, but lapsed into a kind of dreaming that was almost intra-embryonic in lassitude and drowsy vividness. In the faint background the words were spoken, and they wove a tapestry of knowledge in his head.

*

He dreamed of green meadows free of stones, all grass, round and rolling and rushing easily toward a dawn with no taint of freezing, merciless cold or smell of boiled rock or scorched monument. He walked across the green meadow. Overhead the metal seeds flew by in a heaven that was a steady, even temperature. Things were slow, slow, slow.

Birds lingered upon gigantic trees that took a hundred, two hundred, five thousand days to grow. Everything remained in its place, the birds did not flicker nervously at a hint of sun, nor did the trees suck back frightenedly when a ray of sunlight poured over them.

In this dream people strolled, they rarely ran, the heart rhythm of them was evenly languid, not jerking and insane. Their kisses were long and lingering, not the parched mouthings and twitchings of lovers who had eight days to live. The grass remained, and did not burn away in torches. The dream people talked always of tomorrow and living and not tomorrow and dying. It all seemed so familiar that when Sim felt someone take his hand he thought it simply another part of the dream.

Lyte's hand lay inside his own. "Dreaming?" she asked.

"Yes."

"Things are balanced. Our minds, to even things, to balance the unfairness of our living, go back in on ourselves, to find what there is that is good to see."

He beat his hand against the stone floor again and again. "It does not make things fair! I hate it! It reminds me that there is something better, something I have missed! Why can't we be ignorant! Why can't we live and die without knowing that this is an abnormal living?" And his breath rushed harshly from his half-open, constricted mouth.

"There is purpose in everything," said Lyte. "This gives us purpose, makes us work, plan, try to find a way."

His eyes were hot emeralds in his face. "I walked up a hill of grass, very slowly," he said.

"The same hill of grass I walked an hour ago?" asked Lyte.

"Perhaps. Close enough to it. The dream is better than the reality."
He flexed his eyes, narrowed them. "I watched people and they did
not eat."

"Or talk?"

"Or talk, either. And we always are eating, always talking.
Sometimes those people in the dream sprawled with their eyes shut,
not moving a muscle."

As Lyte stared down into his face a terrible thing happened. He
imagined her face blackening, wrinkling, twisting into knots of
agedness. The hair blew out like snow about her ears, the eyes were
like discolored coins caught in a web of lashes. Her teeth sank away
from her lips, the delicate fingers hung like charred twigs from her
atrophied wrists. Her beauty was consumed and wasted even as he
watched, and when he seized her, in terror, he cried out, for he
imagined his own hand corroded, and he choked back a cry.

"Sim, what's wrong?"

The saliva in his mouth dried at the taste of the words.

"Five more days...."

"The Scientists."

Sim started. Who'd spoken? In the dim light a tall man talked.
"The Scientists crashed us on this world, and now have wasted
thousands of lives and time. It's no use. It's no use. Tolerate them
but give them none of your time. You only live once, remember."

Where were these hated Scientists? Now, after the Learning, the
Time of Talking, he was ready to find them. Now, at least, he knew
enough to begin his fight for freedom, for the ship!

"Sim, where're you going?"

But Sim was gone. The echo of his running feet died away down a
shaft of polished stone.

*

THE CREATURES THAT TIME FORGOT

It seemed that half the night was wasted. He blundered into a dozen dead ends. Many times he was attacked by the insane young men who wanted his life energy. Their superstitious ravings echoed after him. The gashes of their hungry fingernails covered his body.

He found what he looked for.

A half dozen men gathered in a small basalt cave deep down in the cliff lode. On a table before them lay objects which, though unfamiliar, struck harmonious chords in Sim.

The Scientists worked in sets, old men doing important work, young men learning, asking questions; and at their feet were three small children. They were a process. Every eight days there was an entirely new set of scientists working on any one problem. The amount of work done was terribly inadequate. They grew old, fell dead just when they were beginning their creative period. The creative time of any one individual was perhaps a matter of twelve hours out of his entire span. Three-quarters of one's life was spent learning, a brief interval of creative power, then senility, insanity, death.

The men turned as Sim entered.

"Don't tell me we have a recruit?" said the eldest of them.

"I don't believe it," said another, younger one. "Chase him away. He's probably one of those war-mongers."

"No, no," objected the elder one, moving with little shuffles of his bare feet toward Sim. "Come in, come in, boy." He had friendly eyes, slow eyes, unlike those of the swift inhabitants of the upper caves. Grey and quiet. "What do you want?"

Sim hesitated, lowered his head, unable to meet the quiet, gentle gaze. "I want to live," he whispered.

The old man laughed quietly. He touched Sim's shoulder. "Are you a new breed? Are you sick?" he queried of Sim, half-seriously. "Why

24

aren't you playing? Why aren't you readying yourself for the time of love and marriage and children? Don't you know that tomorrow night you'll be an adolescent? Don't you realize that if you are not careful you'll miss all of life?" He stopped.

Sim moved his eyes back and forth with each query. He blinked at the instruments on the table top. "Shouldn't I be here?" he asked, naively.

"Certainly," roared the old man, sternly. "But it's a miracle you are. We've had no volunteers from the rank and file for a thousand days! We've had to breed our own scientists, a closed unit! Count us! Six! Six men! And three children! Are we not overwhelming?" The old man spat upon the stone floor. "We ask for volunteers and the people shout back at us, 'Get someone else!' or 'We have no time!' And you know why they say that?"

"No." Sim flinched.

"Because they're selfish. They'd like to live longer, yes, but they know that anything they do cannot possibly insure their *own* lives any extra time. It might guarantee longer life to some future offspring of theirs. But they won't give up their love, their brief youth, give up one interval of sunset or sunrise!"

Sim leaned against the table, earnestly. "I understand."

"You do?" The old man stared at him blindly. He sighed and slapped the child's thigh, gently. "Yes, of course, you do. It's too much to expect anyone to understand, any more. You're rare."

The others moved in around Sim and the old man.

"I am Dienc. Tomorrow night Cort here will be in my place. I'll be dead by then. And the night after that someone else will be in Cort's place, and then you, if you work and believe—but first, I give you a chance. Return to your playmates if you want. There is someone you love? Return to her. Life is short. Why should you care for the unborn to come? You have a right to youth. Go now, if you want. Because if you stay you'll have no time for anything but working and growing old and dying at your work. But it is good work. Well?"

Sim looked at the tunnel. From a distance the wind roared and blew, the smells of cooking and the patter of naked feet sounded, and the laughter of lovers was an increasingly good thing to hear. He shook his head, impatiently, and his eyes were wet.

"I will stay," he said.

*

The third night and third day passed. It was the fourth night. Sim was drawn into their living. He learned about that metal seed upon the top of the far mountain. He heard of the original seeds—things called "ships" that crashed and how the survivors hid and dug in the cliffs, grew old swiftly and in their scrabbling to barely survive, forgot all science. Knowledge of mechanical things had no chance of survival in such a volcanic civilization. There was only NOW for each human.

Yesterday didn't matter, tomorrow stared them vividly in their very faces. But somehow the radiations that had forced their aging had also induced a kind of telepathic communication whereby philosophies and impressions were absorbed by the new born. Racial memory, growing instinctively, preserved memories of another time.

"Why don't we go to that ship on the mountain?" asked Sim.

"It is too far. We would need protection from the sun," explained Dienc.

"Have you tried to make protection?"

"Salves and ointments, suits of stone and bird-wing and, recently, crude metals. None of which worked. In ten thousand more life times perhaps we'll have made a metal in which will flow cool water to protect us on the march to the ship. But we work so slowly, so blindly. This morning, mature, I took up my instruments. Tomorrow, dying, I lay them down. What can one man do in one day? If we had ten thousand men, the problem would be solved...."

"I will go to the ship," said Sim.

"Then you will die," said the old man. A silence had fallen on the room at Sim's words. Then the men stared at Sim. "You are a very selfish boy."

"Selfish!" cried Sim, resentfully.

The old man patted the air. "Selfish in a way I like. You want to live longer, you'll do anything for that. You will try for the ship. But I tell you it is useless. Yet, if you want to, I cannot stop you. At least you will not be like those among us who go to war for an extra few days of life."

"War?" asked Sim. "How can there be war here?"

And a shudder ran through him. He did not understand.

"Tomorrow will be time enough for that," said Dienc. "Listen to me, now."

The night passed.

*

It was morning. Lyte came shouting and sobbing down a corridor, and ran full into his arms. She had changed again. She was older, again, more beautiful. She was shaking and she held to him. "Sim, they're coming after you!"

Bare feet marched down the corridor, surged inward at the opening. Chion stood grinning there, taller, too, a sharp rock in either of his hands. "Oh, there you are, Sim!"

"Go away!" cried Lyte savagely whirling on him.

"Not until we take Sim with us," Chion assured her. Then, smiling at Sim. "*If* that is, he is with us in the fight."

THE CREATURES THAT TIME FORGOT

Dienc shuffled forward, his eye weakly fluttering, his bird-like hands fumbling in the air. "Leave!" he shrilled angrily. "This boy is a Scientist now. He works with us."

Chion ceased smiling. "There is better work to be done. We go now to fight the people in the farthest cliffs." His eyes glittered anxiously. "Of course, you will come with us, Sim?"

"No, no!" Lyte clutched at his arm.

Sim patted her shoulder, then turned to Chion. "Why are you attacking these people?"

"There are three extra days for those who go with us to fight."

"Three extra days! Of living?"

Chion nodded firmly. "If we win, we live eleven days instead of eight. The cliffs they live in, something about the mineral in it! Think of it, Sim, three long, good days of life. Will you join us?"

Dienc interrupted. "Get along without him. Sim is my pupil!"

Chion snorted. "Go die, old man. By sunset tonight you'll be charred bone. Who are you to order us? We are young, we want to live longer."

Eleven days. The words were unbelievable to Sim. Eleven days. Now he understood why there was war. Who wouldn't fight to have his life lengthened by almost half its total. So many more days of youth and love and seeing and living! Yes. Why not, indeed!

"Three extra days," called Dienc, stridently, "*if* you live to enjoy them. If you're not killed in battle. *If. If!* You have never won yet. You have always lost!"

"But this time," Chion declared sharply, "We'll win!"

Sim was bewildered. "But we are all of the same ancestors. Why don't we all share the best cliffs?"

Chion laughed and adjusted a sharp stone in his hand. "Those who live in the best cliffs think they are better than us. That is always man's attitude when he has power. The cliffs there, besides, are smaller, there's room for only three hundred people in them."

Three extra days.

"I'll go with you," Sim said to Chion.

"Fine!" Chion was very glad, much too glad at the decision.

Dienc gasped.

Sim turned to Dienc and Lyte. "If I fight, and win, I will be half a mile closer to the Ship. And I'll have three extra days in which to strive to reach the Ship. That seems the only thing for me to do."

Dienc nodded, sadly. "It *is* the only thing. I believe you. Go along now."

"Good-bye," said Sim.

The old man looked surprised, then he laughed as at a little joke on himself. "That's right—I won't see you again, will I? Good-bye, then." And they shook hands.

They went out, Chion, Sim, and Lyte, together, followed by the others, all children growing swiftly into fighting men. And the light in Chion's eyes was not a good thing to see.

*

Lyte went with him. She chose his rocks for him and carried them. She would not go back, no matter how he pleaded. The sun was just beyond the horizon and they marched across the valley.

"Please, Lyte, go back!"

"And wait for Chion to return?" she said. "He plans that when you die I will be his mate." She shook out her unbelievable blue-white curls of hair defiantly. "But I'll be with you. If you fall, I fall."

Sim's face hardened. He was tall. The world had shrunk during the night. Children packs screamed by hilarious in their food-searching and he looked at them with alien wonder: could it be only four days ago he'd been like these? Strange. There was a sense of many days in his mind, as if he'd really lived a thousand days. There was a dimension of incident and thought so thick, so multi-colored, so richly diverse in his head that it was not to be believed so much could happen in so short a time.

The fighting men ran in clusters of two or three. Sim looked ahead at the rising line of small ebon cliffs. This, then, he said to himself, is my fourth day. And still I am no closer to the Ship, or to anything, not even—he heard the light tread of Lyte beside him—not even to her who bears my weapons and picks me ripe berries.

One-half of his life was gone. Or a third of it—IF he won this battle. *If.*

He ran easily, lifting, letting fall his legs. This is the day of my physical awareness, as I run I feed, as I feed I grow and as I grow I turn eyes to Lyte with a kind of dizzying vertigo. And she looks upon me with the same gentleness of thought. This is the day of our youth. Are we wasting it? Are we losing it on a dream, a folly?

Distantly he heard laughter. As a child he'd questioned it. Now he understood laughter. This particular laughter was made of climbing high rocks and plucking the greenest blades and drinking the headiest vintage from the morning ices and eating of the rock-fruits and tasting of young lips in new appetite.

They neared the cliffs of the enemy.

He saw the slender erectness of Lyte. The new surprise of her white breasts; the neck where if you touched you could time her pulse; the fingers which cupped in your own were animate and supple and never still; the....

Lyte snapped her head to one side. "Look ahead!" she cried. "See what is to come—look only ahead."

He felt that they were racing by part of their lives, leaving their youth on the pathside, without so much as a glance.

"I am blind with looking at stones," he said, running.

"Find new stones, then!"

"I see stones—" His voice grew gentle as the palm of her hand. The landscape floated under him. Everything was like a fine wind, blowing dreamily. "I see stones that make a ravine that lies in a cool shadow where the stone-berries are thick as tears. You touch a boulder and the berries fall in silent red avalanches, and the grass is very tender...."

"I do not see it!" She increased her pace, turning her head away.

He saw the floss upon her neck, like the small moss that grows silvery and light on the cool side of pebbles, that stirs if you breathe the lightest breath upon it. He looked upon himself, his hands clenched as he heaved himself forward toward death. Already his hands were veined and youth-swollen.

They were the hands of a young boy whose fingers are made for touching, which are suddenly sensitive and with more surface, and are nervous, and seem not a part of him because they are so big for the slender lengths of his arms. His neck, through which the blood ached and pumped, was building out with age, too, with tiny blue tendrils of veins imbedded and flaring in it.

Lyte handed him food to eat.

"I am not hungry," he said.

"Eat, keep your mouth full," she commanded sharply. "So you will not talk to me this way!"

"If I could only kiss you," he pleaded. "Just one time."

"After the battle there may be time."

"Gods!" He roared, anguished. "Who cares for battles!"

Ahead of them, rocks hailed down, thudding. A man fell with his skull split wide. The war was begun.

THE CREATURES THAT TIME FORGOT

Lyte passed the weapons to him. They ran without another word until they entered the killing ground. Then he spoke, not looking at her, his cheeks coloring. "Thank you," he said.

She ducked as a slung stone shot by her head. "It was not an easy thing for me," she admitted. "Sim! Be careful!"

The boulders began to roll in a synthetic avalanche from the battlements of the enemy!

*

Only one thought was in his mind now. To kill, to lessen the life of someone else so he could live, to gain a foothold here and live long enough to make a stab at the ship. He ducked, he weaved, he clutched stones and hurled them up. His left hand held a flat stone shield with which he diverted the swiftly plummeting rocks. There was a spatting sound everywhere. Lyte ran with him, encouraging him. Two men dropped before him, slain, their breasts cleaved to the bone, their blood springing out in unbelievable founts.

It was a useless conflict. Sim realized instantly how insane the venture was. They could never storm the cliff. A solid wall of rocks rained down. A dozen men dropped with shards of ebony in their brains, a half dozen more showed drooping, broken arms. One screamed and the upthrust white joint of his knee was exposed as the flesh was pulled away by two successive blows of well-aimed granite. Men stumbled over one another.

The muscles in his cheeks pulled tight and he began to wonder why he had ever come. But his raised eyes, as he danced from side to side, weaving and bobbing, sought always the cliffs. He wanted to live there so intensely, to have his chance. He would have to stick it out. But the heart was gone from him.

Lyte screamed piercingly. Sim, his heart panicking, twisted and saw that her hand was loose at the wrist, with an ugly wound bleeding profusely on the back of the knuckles. She clamped it under her armpit to soothe the pain. The anger rose in him and exploded. In his fury he raced forward, throwing his missiles with deadly accuracy. He saw a man topple and flail down, falling from one level to another of the caves, a victim of his shot. He must have been screaming, for his lungs were bursting open and closed and his throat was raw, and the ground spun madly under his racing feet.

The stone that clipped his head sent him reeling and plunging back. He ate sand. The universe dissolved into purple whorls. He could not get up. He lay and knew that this was his last day, his last time. The battle raged around him, dimly he felt Lyte over him. Her hands cooled his head, she tried to drag him out of range, but he lay gasping and telling her to leave him.

"Stop!" shouted a voice. The whole war seemed to give pause. "Retreat!" commanded the voice swiftly. And as Sim watched, lying upon his side, his comrades turned and fled back toward home.

"The sun is coming, our time is up!" He saw their muscled backs, their moving, tensing, flickering legs go up and down. The dead were left upon the field. The wounded cried for help. But there was no time for the wounded. There was only time for swift men to run the gauntlet home and, their lungs aching and raw with heated air, burst into their tunnels before the sun burnt and killed them.

The sun!

Sim saw another figure racing toward him. It was Chion! Lyte was helping Sim to his feet, whispering helpfully to him. "Can you walk?" she asked. And he groaned and said, "I think so." "Walk then," she said. "Walk slowly, and then faster and faster. We'll make it. Walk slowly, start carefully. We'll make it, I know we will."

Sim got to his feet, stood swaying. Chion raced up, a strange expression cutting lines in his cheeks, his eyes shining with battle.

THE CREATURES THAT TIME FORGOT

Pushing Lyte abruptly aside he seized upon a rock and dealt Sim a jolting blow upon his ankle that laid wide the flesh. All of this was done quite silently.

Now he stood back, still not speaking, grinning like an animal from the night mountains, his chest panting in and out, looking from the thing he had done, to Lyte, and back. He got his breath. "He'll never make it," he nodded at Sim. "We'll have to leave him here. Come along, Lyte."

Lyte, like a cat-animal, sprang upon Chion, searching for his eyes, shrieking through her exposed, hard-pressed teeth. Her fingers stroked great bloody furrows down Chion's arms and again, instantly, down his neck. Chion, with an oath, sprang away from her. She hurled a rock at him. Grunting, he let it miss him, then ran off a few yards. "Fool!" he cried, turning to scorn her. "Come along with me. Sim will be dead in a few minutes. Come along!"

Lyte turned her back on him. "I will go if you carry me."

Chion's face changed. His eyes lost their gleaming. "There is no time. We would both die if I carried you."

Lyte looked through and beyond him. "Carry me, then, for that's how I wish it to be."

Without another word, glancing fearfully at the sun, Chion fled. His footsteps sped away and vanished from hearing. "May he fall and break his neck," whispered Lyte, savagely glaring at his form as it skirted a ravine. She returned to Sim. "Can you walk?"

*

Agonies of pain shot up his leg from the wounded ankle. He nodded ironically. "We could make it to the cave in two hours, walking. I have an idea, Lyte. Carry me." And he smiled with the grim joke.

She took his arm. "Nevertheless we'll walk. Come."

34

"No," he said. "We're staying here."

"But why?"

"We came to seek a home here. If we walk we will die. I would rather die here. How much time have we?"

Together they measured the sun. "A few minutes," she said, her voice flat and dull. She held close to him.

He looked at her. Lyte, he thought. Tomorrow I would have been a man. My body would have been strong and full and there would have been time with you, a kissing and a touching. Damn, but what kind of life is this where every last instant is drenched with fear and alert with death? Am I to be denied even some bit of real life?

The black rocks of the cliff were paling into deep purples and browns as the sun began to flood the world.

What a fool he was! He should have stayed and worked with Dienc, and thought and dreamed, and at least one time cupped Lyte's mouth with his own.

With the sinews of his neck standing out defiantly he bellowed upward at the cliff holes.

"Send me down one man to do battle!"

Silence. His voice echoed from the cliff. The air was warm.

"It's no use," said Lyte, "They'll pay no attention."

He shouted again. "Hear me!" He stood with his weight on his good foot, his injured left leg throbbing and pulsating with pain. He shook a fist. "Send down a warrior who is no coward! I will not turn and run home! I have come to fight a fair fight! Send a man who will fight for the right to his cave! Him I will surely kill!"

More silence. A wave of heat passed over the land, receded.

"Oh, surely," mocked Sim, hands on naked hips, head back, mouth wide, "surely there's one among you not afraid to fight a cripple!" Silence. "No?" Silence.

THE CREATURES THAT TIME FORGOT

"Then I have miscalculated you. I'm wrong. I'll stand here, then, until the sun shucks the flesh off my bone in black scraps, and call you the filthy names you deserve."

He got an answer.

"I do not like being called names," replied a man's voice.

Sim leaned forward, forgetting his crippled foot.

A huge man appeared in a cave mouth on the third level.

"Come down," urged Sim. "Come down, fat one, and kill me."

The man scowled seriously at his opponent a moment, then lumbered slowly down the path, his hands empty of any weapons. Immediately every cave above clustered with heads. An audience for this drama.

The man approached Sim. "We will fight by the rules, if you know them."

"I'll learn as we go," replied Sim.

This pleased the man and he looked at Sim warily, but not unkindly. "This much I will tell you," offered the man generously. "If you die, I will give your mate shelter and she will live, as she pleases, because she is the wife of a good man."

Sim nodded swiftly. "I am ready," he said.

"The rules are simple. We do not touch each other, save with stones. The stones and the sun will do either of us in. Now is the time—"

*

A tip of the sun showed on the horizon. "My name is Nhoj," said Sim's enemy, casually fingering up a handful of pebbles and stones, weighing them. Sim did likewise. He was hungry. He had not eaten for many minutes. Hunger was the curse of this planet's peoples—a perpetual demanding of empty stomachs for more, more food. His blood flushed weakly, shot tinglingly through veins in jolting throbs

36

of heat and pressure, his ribcase shoved out, went in, shoved out again, impatiently.

"Now!" roared the three hundred watchers from the cliffs. "Now!" they clamored, the men and women and children balanced, in turmoil on the ledges. "Now. Begin!"

As if at a cue, the sun leaped high. It smote them a blow as with a flat, sizzling stone. The two men staggered under the molten impact, sweat broke from their naked thighs and loins, under their arms and on their faces was a glaze like fine glass.

Nhoj shifted his huge weight and looked at the sun as if in no hurry to fight. Then, silently, with no warning, he kanurcked out a pebble with a startling trigger-flick of thumb and forefinger. It caught Sim flat on the cheek, staggered him back, so that a rocket of unbearable pain climbed up his crippled foot and burst into nervous explosion at the pit of his stomach. He tasted blood from his bleeding cheek.

Nhoj moved serenely. Three more flickers of his magical hands and three tiny, seemingly harmless bits of stone flew like whistling birds. Each of them found a target, slammed it. The nerve centers of Sim's body! One hit his stomach so that ten hours' eating almost slid up his throat. A second got his forehead, a third his neck. He collapsed to the boiling sand. His knee made a wrenching sound on the hard earth. His face was colorless and his eyes, squeezed tight, were pushing tears out from the hot, quivering lids. But even as he had fallen he had let loose, with wild force, his handful of stones!

The stones purred in the air. One of them, and only one, struck Nhoj. Upon the left eyeball. Nhoj moaned and laid his hands in the next instant to his shattered eye.

Sim choked out a bitter, sighing laugh. This much triumph he had. The eye of his opponent. It would give him ... Time. Oh, gods, he thought, his stomach retching sickly, fighting for breath, this is a world of time. Give me a little more, just a trifle!

Nhoj, one-eyed, weaving with pain, pelted the writhing body of Sim, but his aim was off now, the stones flew to one side or if they struck at all they were weak and spent and lifeless.

Sim forced himself half erect. From the corners of his eyes he saw Lyte, waiting, staring at him, her lips breathing words of encouragement and hope. He was bathed in sweat, as if a rain spray had showered him down.

*

The sun was now fully over the horizon. You could smell it. Stones glinted like mirrors, the sand began to roil and bubble. Illusions sprang up everywhere in the valley. Instead of one warrior Nhoj he was confronted by a dozen, each in an upright position, preparing to launch another missile. A dozen irregular warriors who shimmered in the golden menace of day, like bronze gongs smitten, quivered in one vision!

Sim was breathing desperately. His nostrils flared and sucked and his mouth drank thirstily of flame instead of oxygen. His lungs took fire like silk torches and his body was consumed. The sweat spilled from his pores to be instantly evaporated. He felt himself shriveling, shriveling in on himself, he imagined himself looking like his father, old, sunken, slight, withered! Where was the sand? Could he move? Yes. The world wriggled under him, but now he was on his feet.

There would be no more fighting.

A murmur from the cliff told this. The sunburnt faces of the high audience gaped and jeered and shouted encouragement to their warrior. "Stand straight, Nhoj, save your strength now! Stand tall and perspire!" they urged him. And Nhoj stood, swaying lightly, swaying slowly, a pendulum in an incandescent fiery breath from the skyline. "Don't move, Nhoj, save your heart, save your power!"

"The Test, The Test!" said the people on the heights. "The test of the sun."

And this was the worst part of the fight. Sim squinted painfully at the distorted illusion of cliff. He thought he saw his parents; father with his defeated face, his green eyes burning, mother with her hair blowing like a cloud of grey smoke in the fire wind. He must get up to them, live for and with them!

Behind him, Sim heard Lyte whimper softly. There was a whisper of flesh against sand. She had fallen. He did not dare turn. The strength of turning would bring him thundering down in pain and darkness.

His knees bent. If I fall, he thought, I'll lie here and become ashes. Where was Nhoj? Nhoj was there, a few yards from him, standing bent, slick with perspiration, looking as if he were being hit over the spine with great hammers of destruction.

"Fall, Nhoj! Fall!" screamed Sim, mentally. "Fall, fall! Fall and die so I can take your place!"

But Nhoj did not fall. One by one the pebbles in his half-loose left hand plummeted to the broiling sands and Nhoj's lips peeled back, the saliva burned away from his lips and his eyes glazed. But he did not fall. The will to live was strong in him. He hung as if by a wire.

Sim fell to one knee!

"Ahh!" wailed the knowing voices from the cliff. They were watching death. Sim jerked his head up, smiling mechanically, foolishly as if caught in the act of doing something silly. "No, no," he insisted drowsily, and got back up again. There was so much pain he was all one ringing numbness. A whirring, buzzing, frying sound filled the land. High up, an avalanche came down like a curtain on a drama, making no noise. Everything was quiet except for a steady humming. He saw fifty images of Nhoj now, dressed in armours of sweat, eyes puffed with torture, cheeks sunken, lips peeled back like the rind of a drying fruit. But the wire still held him.

"Now," muttered Sim, sluggishly, with a thick, baked tongue between his blazing teeth. "Now I'll fall and lie and dream." He said it with slow, thoughtful pleasure. He planned it. He knew how it must be done. He would do it accurately. He lifted his head to see if the audience was watching.

They were gone!

The sun had driven them back in. All save one or two brave ones. Sim laughed drunkenly and watched the sweat gather on his dead hands, hesitate, drop off, plunge down toward sand and turn to steam half way there.

Nhoj fell.

The wire was cut. Nhoj fell flat upon his stomach, a gout of blood kicked from his mouth. His eyes rolled back into a white, senseless insanity.

Nhoj fell. So did his fifty duplicate illusions.

All across the valley the winds sang and moaned and Sim saw a blue lake with a blue river feeding it and low white houses near the river with people going and coming in the houses and among the tall green trees. Trees taller than seven men, beside the river mirage.

"Now," explained Sim to himself at last, "Now I can fall. Right—into—that—lake."

He fell forward.

He was shocked when he felt the hands eagerly stop him in midplunge, lift him, hurry him off, high in the hungry air, like a torch held and waved, ablaze.

"How strange is death," he thought, and blackness took him.

*

He wakened to the flow of cool water on his cheeks.

He opened his eyes fearfully. Lyte held his head upon her lap, her fingers were moving food to his mouth. He was tremendously hungry and tired, but fear squeezed both of these things away. He struggled upward, seeing the strange cave contours overhead.

"What time is it?" he demanded.

"The same day as the contest. Be quiet," she said.

"The same day!"

She nodded amusedly. "You've lost nothing of your life. This is Nhoj's cave. We are inside the black cliff. We will live three extra days. Satisfied? Lie down."

"Nhoj is dead?" He fell back, panting, his heart slamming his ribs. He relaxed slowly. "I won. Gods, I won," he breathed.

"Nhoj is dead. So were we, almost. They carried us in from outside only in time."

He ate ravenously. "We have no time to waste. We must get strong. My leg—" He looked at it, tested it. There was a swathe of long yellow grasses around it and the ache had died away. Even as he watched the terrific pulsings of his body went to work and cured away the impurities under the bandages. It *has* to be strong by sunset, he thought. It *has* to be.

He got up and limped around the cave like a captured animal. He felt Lyte's eyes upon him. He could not meet her gaze. Finally, helplessly, he turned.

She interrupted him. "You want to go on to the ship?" she asked, softly. "Tonight? When the sun goes down?"

He took a breath, exhaled it. "Yes."

"You couldn't possibly wait until morning?"

"No."

THE CREATURES THAT TIME FORGOT

"Then I'll go with you."

"No!"

"If I lag behind, let me. There's nothing here for me."

They stared at each other a long while. He shrugged wearily.

"All right," he said, at last. "I couldn't stop you, I know that. We'll go together."

*

They waited in the mouth of their new cave. The sun set. The stones cooled so that one could walk on them. It was almost time for the leaping out and the running toward the distant, glittering metal seed that lay on the far mountain.

Soon would come the rains. And Sim thought back over all the times he had watched the rains thicken into creeks, into rivers that cut new beds each night. One night there would be a river running north, the next a river running north-east, the third night a river running due west. The valley was continually cut and scarred by the torrents. Earthquakes and avalanches filled the old beds. New ones were the order of the day. It was this idea of the river and the directions of the river that he had turned over in his head for many hours. It might possibly—Well, he would wait and see.

He noticed how living in this new cliff had slowed his pulse, slowed everything. A mineral result, protection against the solar radiations. Life was still swift, but not as swift as before.

"Now, Sim!" cried Lyte, testing the valley air.

They ran. Between the hot death and the cold one. Together, away from the cliffs, out toward the distant, beckoning ship.

Never had they run this way in their lives. The sound of their feet running was a hard, insistent clatter over vast oblongs of rock, down into ravines, up the sides, and on again. They raked the air in and out their lungs. Behind them the cliffs faded away into things they could never turn back to now.

They did not eat as they ran. They had eaten to the bursting point in the cave, to save time. Now it was only running, a lifting of legs, a balancing of bent elbows, a convulsion of muscles, a slaking in of air that had been fiery and was now cooling.

"Are they watching us?"

Lyte's breathless voice snatched at his ears, above the pound of his heart.

Who? But he knew the answer. The cliff peoples, of course. How long had it been since a race like this one? A thousand days? Ten thousand? How long since someone had taken the chance and sprinted with an entire civilization's eyes upon their backs, into gullies, across cooling plain. Were there lovers pausing in their laughter back there, gazing at the two tiny dots that were a man and woman running toward destiny? Were children eating of new fruits and stopping in their play to see the two people racing against time? Was Dienc still living, narrowing hairy eyebrows down over fading eyes, shouting them on in a feeble, rasping voice, shaking a twisted hand? Were there jeers? Were they being called fools, idiots? And in the midst of the name calling, were people praying them on, hoping they would reach the ship? Yes, under all the cynicism and pessimism, some of them, all of them, must be praying.

Sim took a quick glance at the sky, which was beginning to bruise with the coming night. Out of nowhere clouds materialized and a light shower trailed across a gully two hundred yards ahead of them. Lightning beat upon distant mountains and there was a strong scent of ozone on the disturbed air.

THE CREATURES THAT TIME FORGOT

"The halfway mark," panted Sim, and he saw Lyte's face half turn, longingly looking back at the life she was leaving. "Now's the time, if we want to turn back, we still have time. Another minute—"

*

Thunder snarled in the mountains. An avalanche started out small and ended up huge and monstrous in a deep fissure. Light rain dotted Lyte's smooth white skin. In a minute her hair was glistening and soggy with rain.

"Too late now," she shouted over the patting rhythm of her own naked feet. "We've got to go ahead!"

And it was too late. Sim knew, judging the distances, that there was no turning back now.

His leg began to pain him a little. He favored it, slowing. A wind came up swiftly. A cold wind that bit into the skin. But it came from the cliffs behind them, helped rather than hindered them. An omen? he wondered. No.

For as the minutes went by it grew upon him how poorly he had estimated the distance. Their time was dwindling out, but they were still an impossible distance from the ship. He said nothing, but the impotent anger at the slow muscles in his legs welled up into bitterly hot tears in his eyes.

He knew that Lyte was thinking the same as himself. But she flew along like a white bird, seeming hardly to touch ground. He heard her breath go out and in her throat, like a clean, sharp knife in its sheathe.

Half the sky was dark. The first stars were peering through lengths of black cloud. Lightning jiggled a path along a rim just ahead of them. A full thunderstorm of violent rain and exploding electricity fell upon them.

They slipped and skidded on moss-smooth pebbles. Lyte fell, scrambled up again with a burning oath. Her body was scarred and dirty. The rain washed over her.

The rain came down and cried on Sim. It filled his eyes and ran in rivers down his spine and he wanted to cry with it.

Lyte fell and did not rise, sucking her breath, her breasts quivering.

He picked her up and held her. "Run, Lyte, please, run!"

"Leave me, Sim. Go ahead!" The rain filled her mouth. There was water everywhere. "It's no use. Go on without me."

He stood there, cold and powerless, his thoughts sagging, the flame of hope blinking out. All the world was blackness, cold falling sheaths of water, and despair.

"We'll walk, then," he said. "And keep walking, and resting."

They walked for fifty yards, easily, slowly, like children out for a stroll. The gully ahead of them filled with water that went sliding away with a swift wet sound, toward the horizon.

Sim cried out. Tugging at Lyte he raced forward. "A new channel," he said, pointing. "Each day the rain cuts a new channel. Here, Lyte!" He leaned over the flood waters.

He dived in, taking her with him.

The flood swept them like bits of wood. They fought to stay upright, the water got into their mouths, their noses. The land swept by on both sides of them. Clutching Lyte's fingers with insane strength, Sim felt himself hurled end over end, saw flicks of lightning on high, and a new fierce hope was born in him. They could no longer run, well, then they would let the water do the running for them.

With a speed that dashed them against rocks, split open their shoulders, abraded their legs, the new, brief river carried them. "This way!" Sim shouted over a salvo of thunder and steered frantically toward the opposite side of the gully. The mountain where the ship lay was just ahead. They must not pass it by. They fought in the transporting liquid and were slammed against the far side. Sim leaped up, caught at an overhanging rock, locked Lyte in his legs, and drew himself hand over hand upward.

As quickly as it had come, the storm was gone. The lightning faded. The rain ceased. The clouds melted and fell away over the sky. The wind whispered into silence.

"The ship!" Lyte lay upon the ground. "The ship, Sim. This is the mountain of the ship!"

Now the cold came. The killing cold.

They forced themselves drunkenly up the mountain. The cold slid along their limbs, got into their arteries like a chemical and slowed them.

Ahead of them, with a fresh-washed sheen, lay the ship. It was a dream. Sim could not believe that they were actually so near it. Two hundred yards. One hundred and seventy yards. Gods, but it was cold.

The ground became covered with ice. They slipped and fell again and again. Behind them the river was frozen into a blue-white snake of cold solidity. A few last drops of rain from somewhere came down as hard pellets.

Sim fell against the bulk of the ship. He was actually touching it. Touching it! He heard Lyte whimpering in her constricted throat. This was the metal, the ship. How many others had touched it in the long days? He and Lyte had made it!

He touched it lovingly. Then, as cold as the air, his veins were chilled.

Where was the entrance?

RAY BRADBURY

You run, you swim, you almost drown, you curse, you sweat, you work, you reach a mountain, you go up it, you hammer on metal, you shout with relief, you reach the ship, and then—you can't find the entrance.

*

He fought to keep himself from breaking down. Slowly, he told himself, but not too slowly, go around the ship. The metal slid under his searching hands, so cold that his hands, sweating, almost froze to it. Now, far around to the side. Lyte moved with him. The cold held them like a fist. It began to squeeze.

The entrance.

Metal. Cold, immutable metal. A thin line of opening at the sealing point. Throwing all caution aside, he beat at it. He felt his stomach seething with cold. His fingers were numb, his eyes were half frozen in their sockets. He began to beat and search and scream against the metal door. "Open up! Open up!" He staggered.

The air-lock sighed. With a whispering of metal on rubber beddings, the door swung softly sidewise and vanished back.

He saw Lyte run forward, clutch at her throat, and drop inside a small shiny chamber. He shuffled after her, blankly.

The air-lock door sealed shut behind him.

He could not breathe. His heart began to slow, to stop.

They were trapped inside the ship now, and something was happening. He sank down to his knees and choked for air.

The ship he had come to for salvation was now slowing his pulse, darkening his brain, poisoning him. With a starved, faint kind of expiring terror, he realized that he was dying.

Blackness.

*

47

THE CREATURES THAT TIME FORGOT

He had a dim sense of time passing, of thinking, struggling, to make his heart go quick, quick.... To make his eyes focus. But the fluid in his body lagged quietly through his settling veins and he heard his temple pulses thud, pause, thud, pause and thud again with lulling intermissions.

He could not move, not a hand or leg or finger. It was an effort to lift the tonnage of his eyelashes. He could not shift his face even, to see Lyte lying beside him.

From a distance came her irregular breathing. It was like the sound a wounded bird makes with his dry, unraveled pinions. She was so close he could almost feel the heat of her; yet she seemed a long way removed.

I'm getting cold! he thought. Is this death? This slowing of blood, of my heart, this cooling of my body, this drowsy thinking of thoughts?

Staring at the ship's ceiling he traced its intricate system of tubes and machines. The knowledge, the purpose of the ship, its actions, seeped into him. He began to understand in a kind of revealing lassitude just what these things were his eyes rested upon. Slow. Slow.

There was an instrument with a gleaming white dial.

Its purpose?

He drudged away at the problem, like a man underwater.

People had used the dial. Touched it. People had repaired it. Installed it. People had dreamed of it before the building, before the installing, before the repairing and touching and using. The dial contained memory of use and manufacture, its very shape was a dream-memory telling Sim why and for what it had been built. Given time, looking at anything, he could draw from it the knowledge he desired. Some dim part of him reached out, dissected the contents of things, analyzed them.

RAY BRADBURY

This dial measured time!

Millions of days of time!

But how could that be? Sim's eyes dilated, hot and glittering. Where were humans who needed such an instrument?

Blood thrummed and beat behind his eyes. He closed them.

Panic came to him. The day was passing. I am lying here, he thought, and my life slips away. I cannot move. My youth is passing. How long before I can move?

Through a kind of porthole he saw the night pass, the day come, the day pass, and again another night. Stars danced frostily.

I will lie here for four or five days, wrinkling and withering, he thought. This ship will not let me move. How much better if I had stayed in my home cliff, lived, enjoyed this short life. What good has it done to come here? I'm missing all the twilights and dawns. I'll never touch Lyte, though she's here at my side.

Delirium. His mind floated up. His thoughts whirled through the metal ship. He smelled the razor sharp smell of joined metal. He heard the hull contract with night, relax with day.

Dawn.

Already—another dawn!

Today I would have been mature. His jaw clenched. I must get up. I must move. I must enjoy my time of maturity.

But he didn't move. He felt his blood pump sleepily from chamber to red chamber in his heart, on down and around through his dead body, to be purified by his folding and unfolding lungs. Then the circuit once more.

The ship grew warm. From somewhere a machine clicked. Automatically the temperature cooled. A controlled gust of air flushed the room.

Night again. And then another day.

THE CREATURES THAT TIME FORGOT

He lay and saw four days of his life pass.

He did not try to fight. It was no use. His life was over.

He didn't want to turn his head now. He didn't want to see Lyte with her face like his tortured mother's—eyelids like gray ash flakes, eyes like beaten, sanded metal, cheeks like eroded stones. He didn't want to see a throat like parched thongs of yellow grass, hands the pattern of smoke risen from a fire, breasts like desiccated rinds and hair stubbly and unshorn as moist gray weeds!

And himself? How did *he* look? Was his jaw sunken, the flesh of his eyes pitted, his brow lined and age-scarred?

*

His strength began to return. He felt his heart beating so slow that it was amazing. One hundred beats a minute. Impossible. He felt so cool, so thoughtful, so easy.

His head fell over to one side. He stared at Lyte. He shouted in surprise.

She was young and fair.

She was looking at him, too weak to say anything. Her eyes were like tiny silver medals, her throat curved like the arm of a child. Her hair was blue fire eating at her scalp, fed by the slender life of her body.

Four days had passed and still she was young ... no, younger than when they had entered the ship. She was still adolescent.

He could not believe it.

Her first words were, "How long will this last?"

He replied, carefully. "I don't know."

"We are still young."

"The ship. Its metal is around us. It cuts away the sun and the things that came from the sun to age us."

Her eyes shifted thoughtfully. "Then, if we stay here—"

"We'll remain young."

"Six more days? Fourteen more? Twenty?"

"More than that, maybe."

She lay there, silently. After a long time she said, "Sim?"

"Yes."

"Let's stay here. Let's not go back. If we go back now, you know what'll happen to us...?"

"I'm not certain."

"We'll start getting old again, won't we?"

He looked away. He stared at the ceiling and the clock with the moving finger. "Yes. We'll grow old."

"What if we grow old—instantly. When we step from the ship won't the shock be too much?"

"Maybe."

Another silence. He began to move his limbs, testing them. He was very hungry. "The others are waiting," he said.

Her next words made him gasp. "The others are dead," she said. "Or will be in a few hours. All those we knew back there are old and worn."

He tried to picture them old. Dark, his sister, bent and senile with time. He shook his head, wiping the picture away. "They may die," he said. "But there are others who've been born."

"People we don't even know," said Lyte, flatly.

"But, nevertheless, *our* people," he replied. "People who'll live only eight days, or eleven days unless we help them."

"But we're *young*, Sim! We're young! We can *stay* young!"

He didn't want to listen. It was too tempting a thing to listen to. To stay here. To live. "We've already had more time than the others," he said. "I need workers. Men to heal this ship. We'll get on our feet now, you and I, and find food, eat, and see if the ship is movable. I'm afraid to try to move it myself. It's so big. I'll need help."

"But that means running back all that distance!"

"I know." He lifted himself weakly. "But I'll do it."

"How will you get the men back here?"

"We'll use the river."

"*If* it's there. It *may* be somewhere else."

"We'll wait until there *is* one, then. I've got to go back, Lyte. The son of Dienc is waiting for me, my sister, your brother, are old people, ready to die, and waiting for some word from us—"

After a long while he heard her move, dragging herself tiredly to him. She put her head upon his chest, her eyes closed, stroking his arm. "I'm sorry. Forgive me. You have to go back. I'm a selfish fool."

He touched her cheek, clumsily. "You're human. I understand you. There's nothing to forgive."

*

They found food. They walked through the ship. It was empty. Only in the control room did they find the remains of a man who must have been the chief pilot. The others had evidently bailed out into space in emergency lifeboats. This pilot, sitting at his controls, alone, had landed the ship on a mountain within sight of other fallen and smashed crafts. Its location on high ground had saved it from the floods. The pilot himself had died, probably of heart failure, soon after landing. The ship had remained here, almost within reach of the other survivors, perfect as an egg, but silent, for—how many thousand days? If the pilot had lived, what a different thing life might have been for the ancestors of Sim and Lyte. Sim, thinking of this—felt the distant, ominous vibration of war. How had the war between worlds come out? Who had won? Or had both planets lost and never bothered trying to pick up survivors? Who had been right?

Who was the enemy? Were Sim's people of the guilty or innocent side? They might never know.

He checked the ship hurriedly. He knew nothing of its workings, yet as he walked its corridors, patted its machines, he learned from it. It needed only a crew. One man couldn't possibly set the whole thing running again. He laid his hand upon one round, snout-like machine. He jerked his hand away, as if burnt.

"Lyte!"

"What is it?"

He touched the machine again, caressed it, his hand trembled violently, his eyes welled with tears, his mouth opened and closed, he looked at the machine, loving it, then looked at Lyte.

"With this machine—" he stammered, softly, incredulously. "With—with this machine I can—"

"What, Sim?"

He inserted his hand into a cup-like contraption with a lever inside. Out of porthole in front of him he could see the distant line of cliffs. "We were afraid there might never be another river running by this mountain, weren't we?" he asked, exultantly.

"Yes, Sim, but—"

"There *will* be a river. And I *will* come back, tonight! And I'll bring men with me. Five hundred men! Because with this machine I can blast a river bottom all the way to the cliffs, down which the waters will rush, giving myself and the men a swift, sure way of traveling back!" He rubbed the machine's barrel-like body. "When I touched it, the life and method of it shot into me! Watch!" He depressed the lever.

A beam of incandescent fire lanced out from the ship, screaming.

Steadily, accurately, Sim began to cut away a river bed for the storm waters to flow in. The night was turned to day by its hungry eating.

THE CREATURES THAT TIME FORGOT

*

The return to the cliffs was to be carried out by Sim alone. Lyte was to remain in the ship, in case of any mishap. The trip back seemed, at first glance, to be impossible. There would be no river rushing to cut his time, to sweep him along toward his destination. He would have to run the entire distance in the dawn, and the sun would get him, catch him before he'd reached safety.

"The only way to do it is to start *before* sunrise."

"But you'd be frozen, Sim."

"Here." He made adjustments on the machine that had just finished cutting the river bed in the rock floor of the valley. He lifted the smooth snout of the gun, pressed the lever, left it down. A gout of fire shot toward the cliffs. He fingered the range control, focused the flame end three miles from its source. Done. He turned to Lyte. "But I don't understand," she said.

He opened the air-lock door. "It's bitter cold out, and half an hour yet till dawn. If I run parallel to the flame from the machine, close enough to it, there'll not be much heat but enough to sustain life, anyway."

"It doesn't sound safe," Lyte protested.

"*Nothing* does, on this world." He moved forward. "I'll have a half hour start. That should be enough to reach the cliffs."

"But if the machine should fail while you're still running near its beam?"

"Let's not think of that," he said.

A moment later he was outside. He staggered as if kicked in the stomach. His heart almost exploded in him. The environment of his world forced him into swift living again. He felt his pulse rise, kicking through his veins.

The night was cold as death. The heat ray from the ship sliced across the valley, humming, solid and warm. He moved next to it, very close. One misstep in his running and—

"I'll be back," he called to Lyte.

He and the ray of light went together.

*

In the early morning the peoples in the caves saw the long finger of orange incandescence and the weird whitish apparition floating, running along beside it. There was muttering and superstition.

So when Sim finally reached the cliffs of his childhood he saw alien peoples swarming there. There were no familiar faces. Then he realized how foolish it was to expect familiar faces. One of the older men glared down at him. "Who're you?" he shouted. "Are you from the enemy cliff? What's your name?"

"I am Sim, the son of Sim!"

"Sim!"

An old woman shrieked from the cliff above him. She came hobbling down the stone pathway. "Sim, Sim, it *is* you!"

He looked at her, frankly bewildered. "But I don't know you," he murmured.

"Sim, don't you recognize me? Oh, Sim, it's me! Dark!"

"Dark!"

He felt sick at his stomach. She fell into his arms. This old, trembling woman with the half-blind eyes, his sister.

Another face appeared above. That of an old man. A cruel, bitter face. It looked down at Sim and snarled. "Drive him away!" cried the old man. "He comes from the cliff of the enemy. He's lived there! He's still young! Those who go there can never come back among us. Disloyal beast!" And a rock hurtled down.

Sim leaped aside, pulling the old woman with him.

THE CREATURES THAT TIME FORGOT

A roar came from the people. They ran toward Sim, shaking their fists. "Kill him, kill him!" raved the old man, and Sim did not know who he was.

"Stop!" Sim held out his hands. "I come from the ship!"

"The ship?" The people slowed. Dark clung to him, looking up into his young face, puzzling over its smoothness.

"Kill him, kill him, kill him!" croaked the old man, and picked up another rock.

"I offer you ten days, twenty days, thirty more days of life!"

The people stopped. Their mouths hung open. Their eyes were incredulous.

"Thirty days?" It was repeated again and again. "How?"

"Come back to the ship with me. Inside it, one can live forever!"

The old man lifted high a rock, then, choking, fell forward in an apoplectic fit, and tumbled down the rocks to lie at Sim's feet.

Sim bent to peer at the ancient one, at the bleary, dead eyes, the loose, sneering lips, the crumpled, quiet body.

"Chion!"

"Yes," said Dark behind him, in a croaking, strange voice. "Your enemy. Chion."

*

That night a thousand warriors started for the ship as if going to war. The water ran in the new channel. Five hundred of them were drowned or lost behind in the cold. The others, with Sim, got through to the ship.

Lyte awaited them, and threw wide the metal door.

The weeks passed. Generations lived and died in the cliffs, while the five hundred workers labored over the ship, learning its functions and its parts.

RAY BRADBURY

On the last day they disbanded. Each ran to his station. Now there was a destiny of travel who still remained behind.

Sim touched the control plates under his fingers.

Lyte, rubbing her eyes, came and sat on the floor next to him, resting her head against his knee, drowsily. "I had a dream," she said, looking off at something far away. "I dreamed I lived in caves in a cliff on a cold-hot planet where people grew old and died in eight days and were burnt."

"What an impossible dream," said Sim. "People couldn't possibly live in such a nightmare. Forget it. You're awake now."

He touched the plates gently. The ship rose and moved into space. Sim was right. The nightmare was over at last.

www.ingramcontent.com/pod-product-compliance
Lightning Source LLC
Chambersburg PA
CBHW030542180626
46810CB00005B/1976